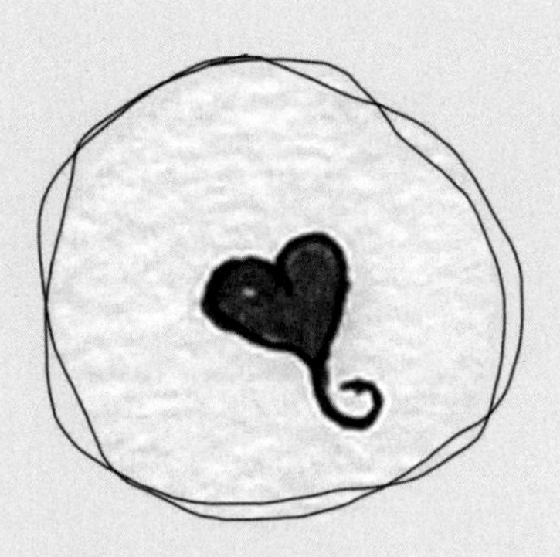

This book is dedicated to my favorite little one with a huge imagination...I love you every cup of tea in the world. To my husband for his never-ceasing love and patience through all of my work...You are the jam on my scone. To my parents who have believed in every creative thing I've ever done...The fans for my flame.

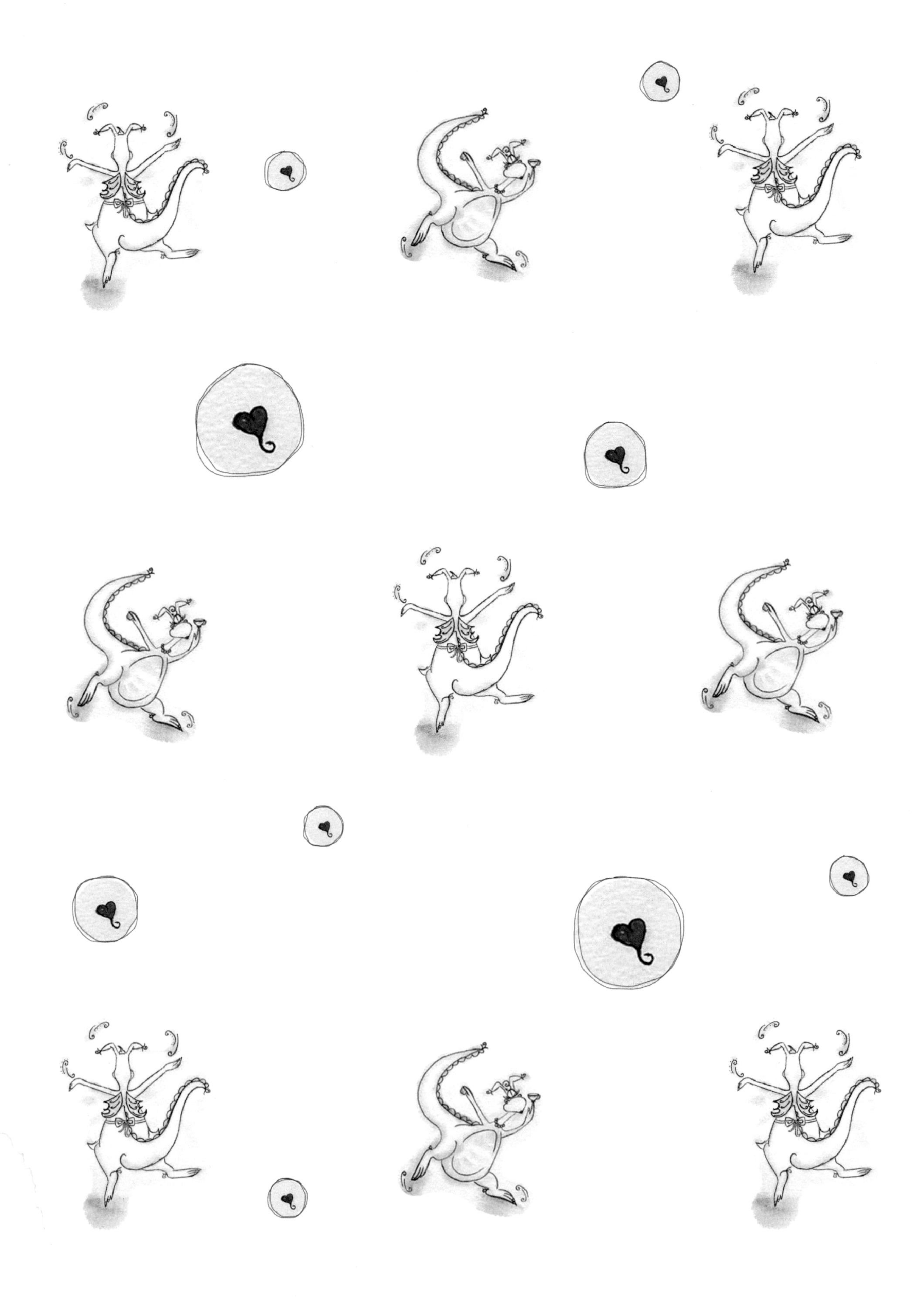

Dear Enoch,
Beulah, Elijah.
May you be brave, be
kind & have beautiful
adventures!
♡
Sara E

Dragons really do Love TEA

Written and Illustrated
by Sara Ernst

Dragons Really Do Love Tea

ISBN-13: 978-1545473221

There once was a mountain with a deep, dark cave.
There once was a girl who was extremely brave.

She had heard in that dwelling there lived something fierce
With long, sharp teeth and claws that pierce.

With scales that lay upon its shoulders and
Flaring nostrils large as boulders.

The townsfolk said these were not lies,
That what was inside had wings to fly.

She would see for herself since no one had tried.
"Don't go!" they cried. "There's a dragon inside!"

But she packed her things and was on her way,
It was a bright and warm and cheery day.

"Nothing that fierce could live so near,"
She said as she walked. "I will not fear!"

Three days she walked, two days she climbed
With songs she sang to pass the time.

Just as she made it to the top,
From the mouth of the cave came a **Puff**

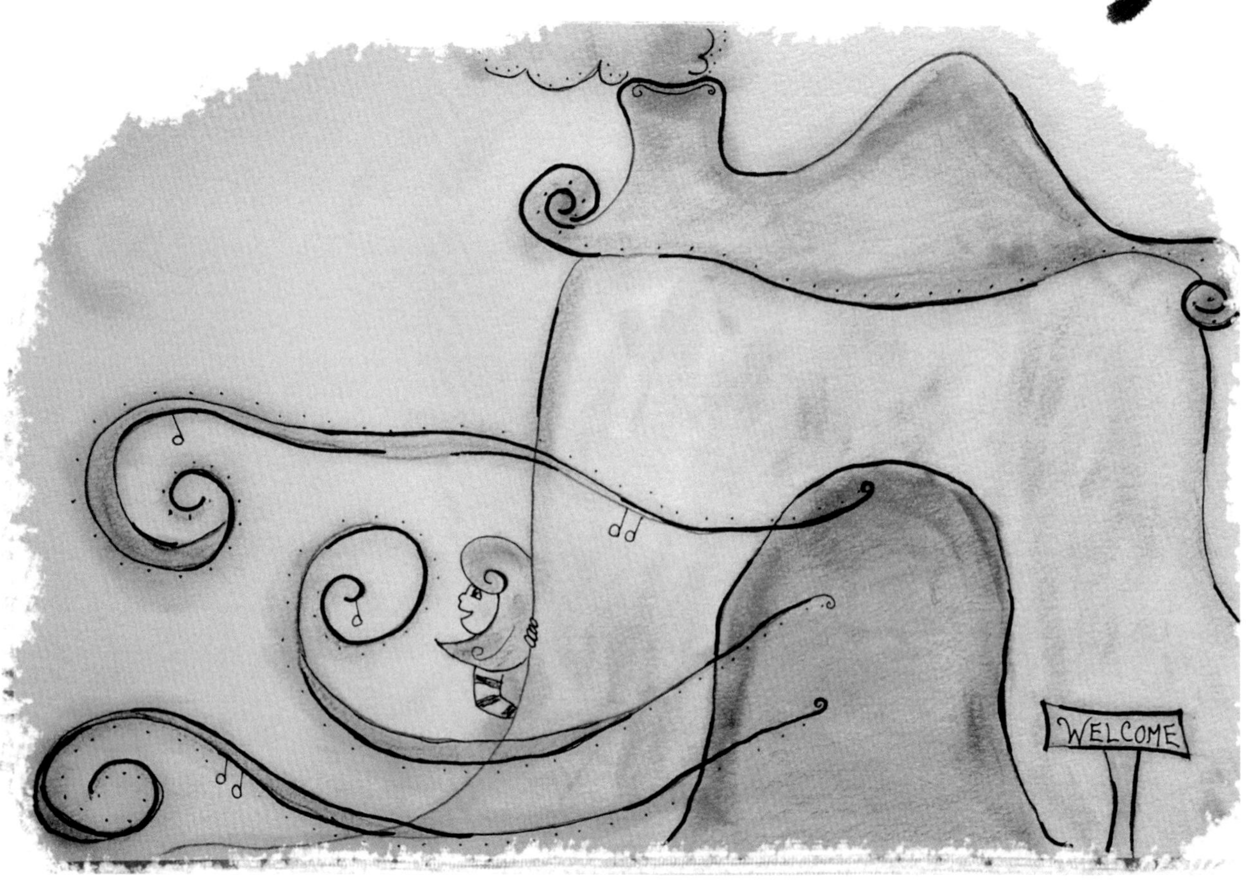

and a **POP**

Smoke was swirling everywhere
Around her clothes and through her hair...

And what was that sound? It wasn't scary.
It was lovely, homey, sweet, and merry.

Deeper inside she crept oh so slow,
What or who lived there she had to know.

She came to a corner and around she peeked,
It WAS a dragon...and...she was having TEA?

The smell of butter, jam, and scones
Wafted through the cave of stone.

The dragon turned and saw the girl!
At first she was startled, but then she twirled...

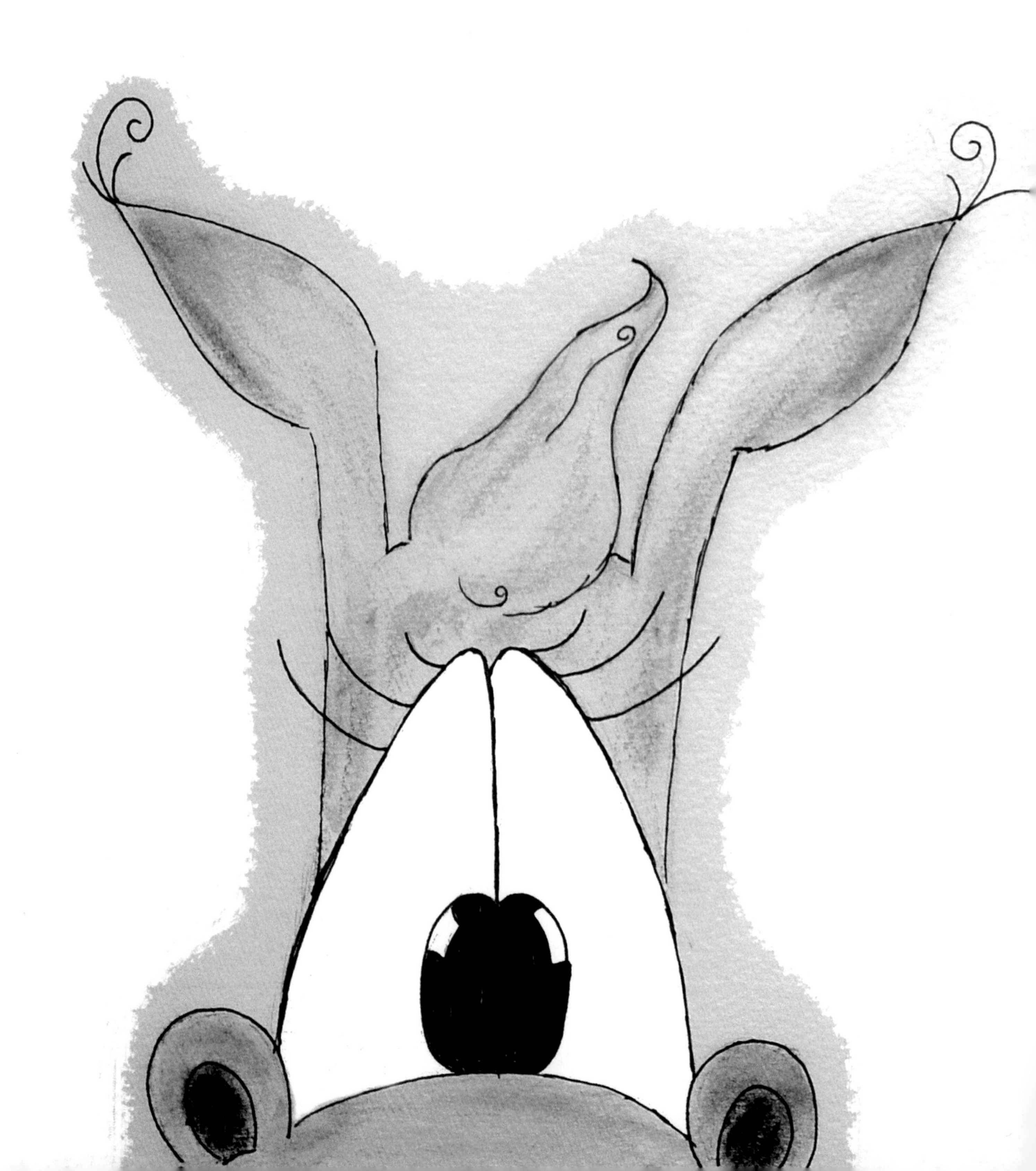

"Oh, hello dear!" she squealed with glee.
"How I've always wanted someone over for tea!"

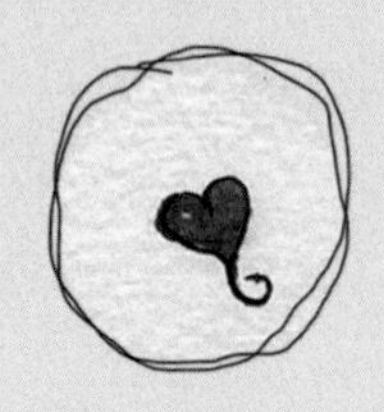

"I'll just warm up the water so it's hot!"

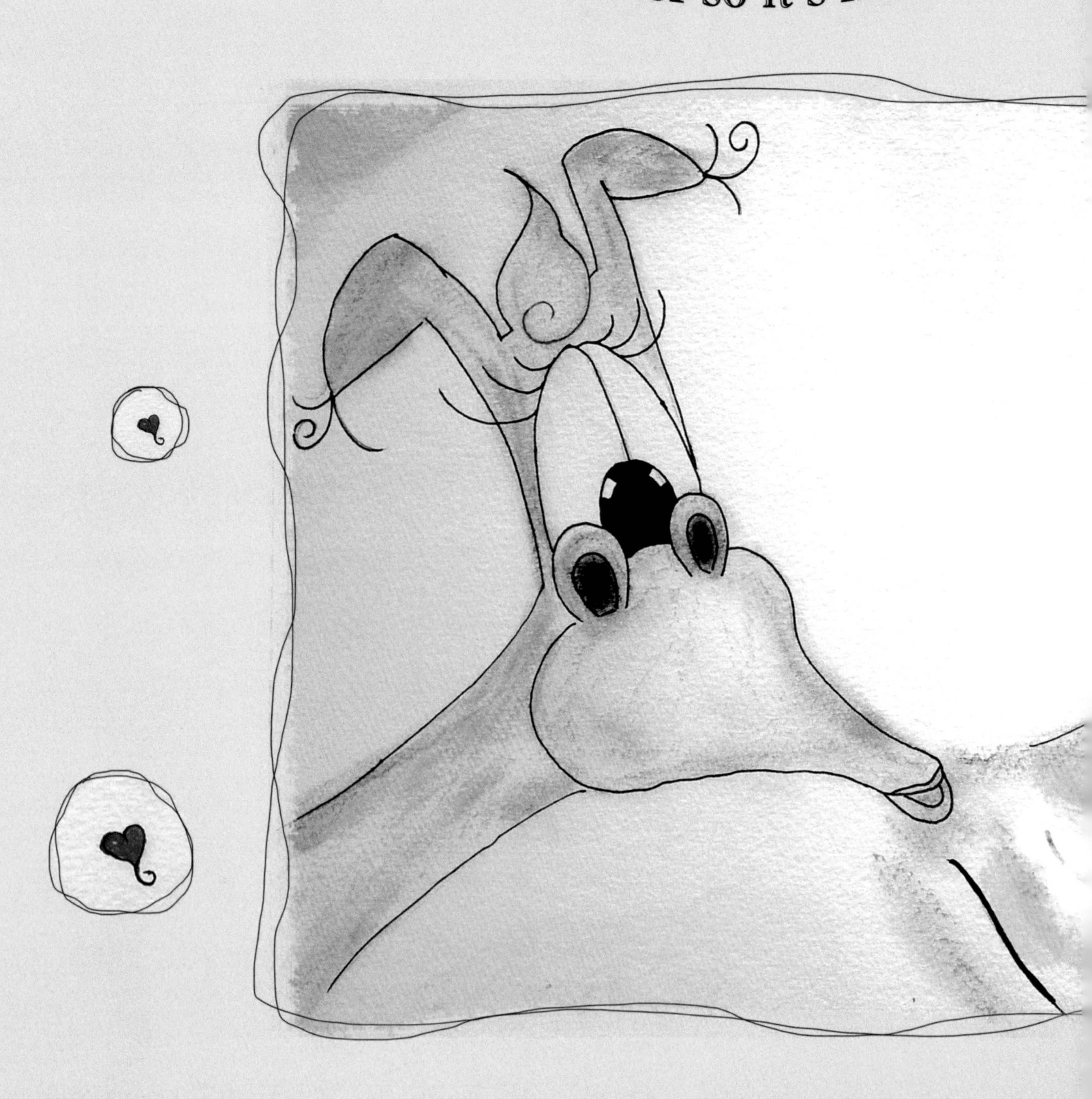

Then she breathed fire around the pot.

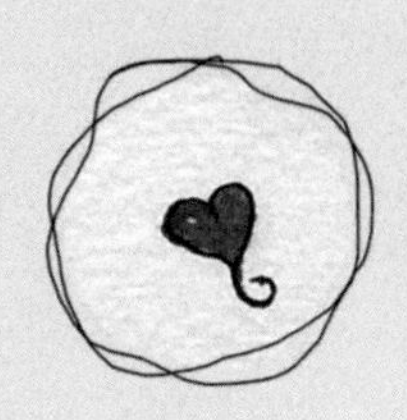

"Oh, my day is made! Sit here! Sit here!

Thank you so much for coming to visit, my dear!"

She took off her apron

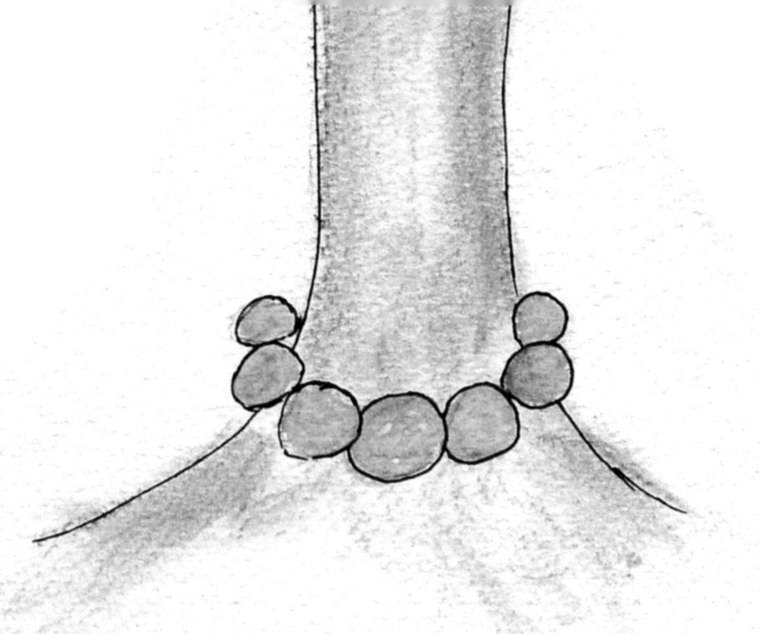

And put on some pearls

“Being a dragon is hard,” she sighed.
“Everyone fears me no matter how hard I try.”

“Well, they just don’t know you!” said the girl cheerfully.
“Why, I had no idea that dragons liked tea.”

“Oh, I love tea and dancing, to sing, and to bake,
I love cozy blankets, books, and cake!”

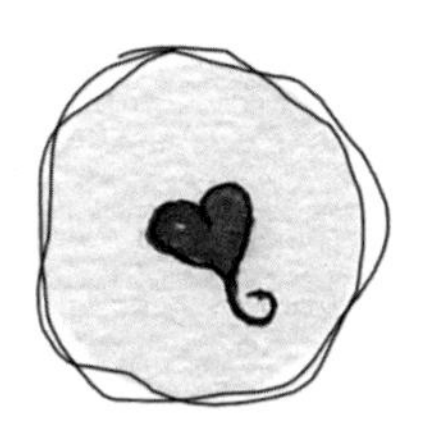

The girl bit into a scone, and oh how divine,
"These scones," the girl said, "are the finest of fine!"

"You could make these," she said, "for the people in town,
I'm sure that would turn their opinions around."

"Do you think?" the dragon asked kindly.
"Do you think things could change?

Then in a sweet puff of smoke the dragon started to dance.

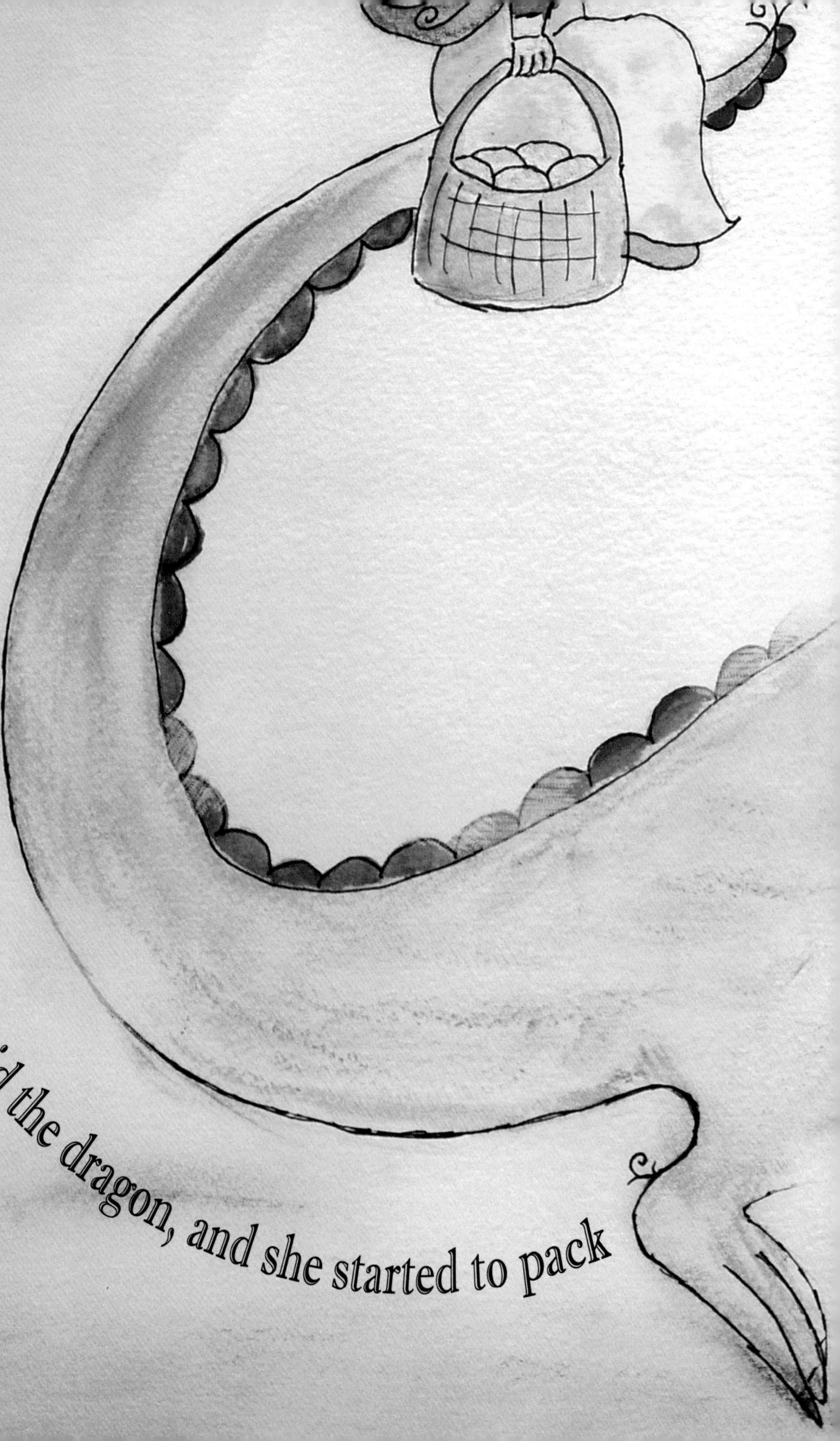

"Let's go now!" said the dragon, and she started to pack

"You can hold the basket and fly on my back!"

So down they flew to the town below,
But the townsfolk were running to and fro.

“Wait!” cried the girl. “You’ve had it ALL wrong!
This dragon is kind...she bakes and sings songs!”

They tried the scones and shared some tea,
Such a happy event it was to see.

Down the dragon's cheek ran long, kind tears
As the town apologized for thinking her fierce.

So the town found a dragon and the dragon a town
And the girl and the dragon, best friends all around.

You might not believe it,
but I assure you, dear friends...

Dragons really do love tea. And that, is
THE END.

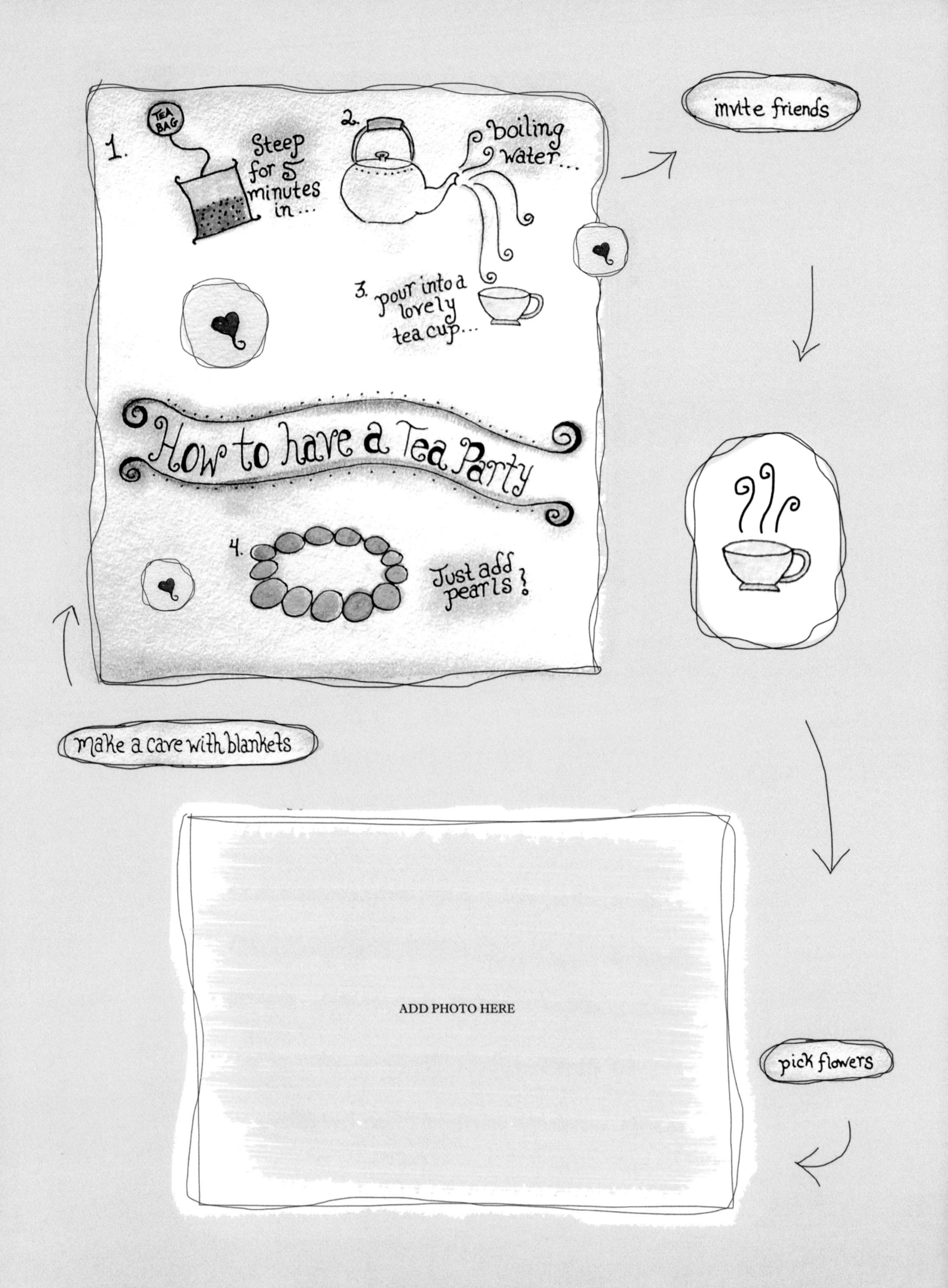
TEA BAG
1.
Steep for 5 minutes in...
2.
boiling water...
3. pour into a lovely tea cup...
How to have a Tea Party
4.
Just add pearls?
invite friends
make a cave with blankets
ADD PHOTO HERE
pick flowers

Dragon Scones
an allergy-friendly scone that is
gluten, dairy, nut, egg, refined sugar-free
1/2c • old-fashioned oats
1/4c • tapioca flour
1/4c • white rice flour
1/4 tsp • baking soda
1/8 tsp • vanilla
1 tbsp • maple syrup
2 tbsp • coconut oil (solid)
10 tsp • rice milk (unsweetened)
Mix with hands until even. Form into 6 balls; flatten slightly; put on a parchment-lined cookie pan. Bake at 350°F for 15 minutes.
add raisins, chocolate chips or more maple for a sweeter scone.

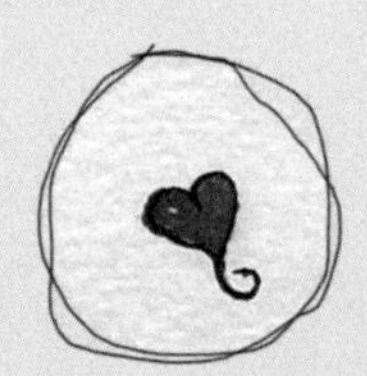

When she isn't photographing children and families, you might find Sara Ernst writing stories for them. She has had a love for children since she was a child herself and is happy to admit that she has never completely grown up. One thing is for certain, if there is a pen in one hand...there is a cup of tea in the other.

For more information on her work as a photographer, visit
www.saraernst.com

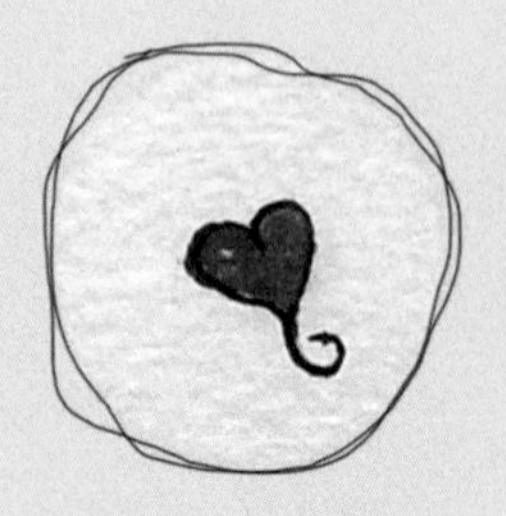

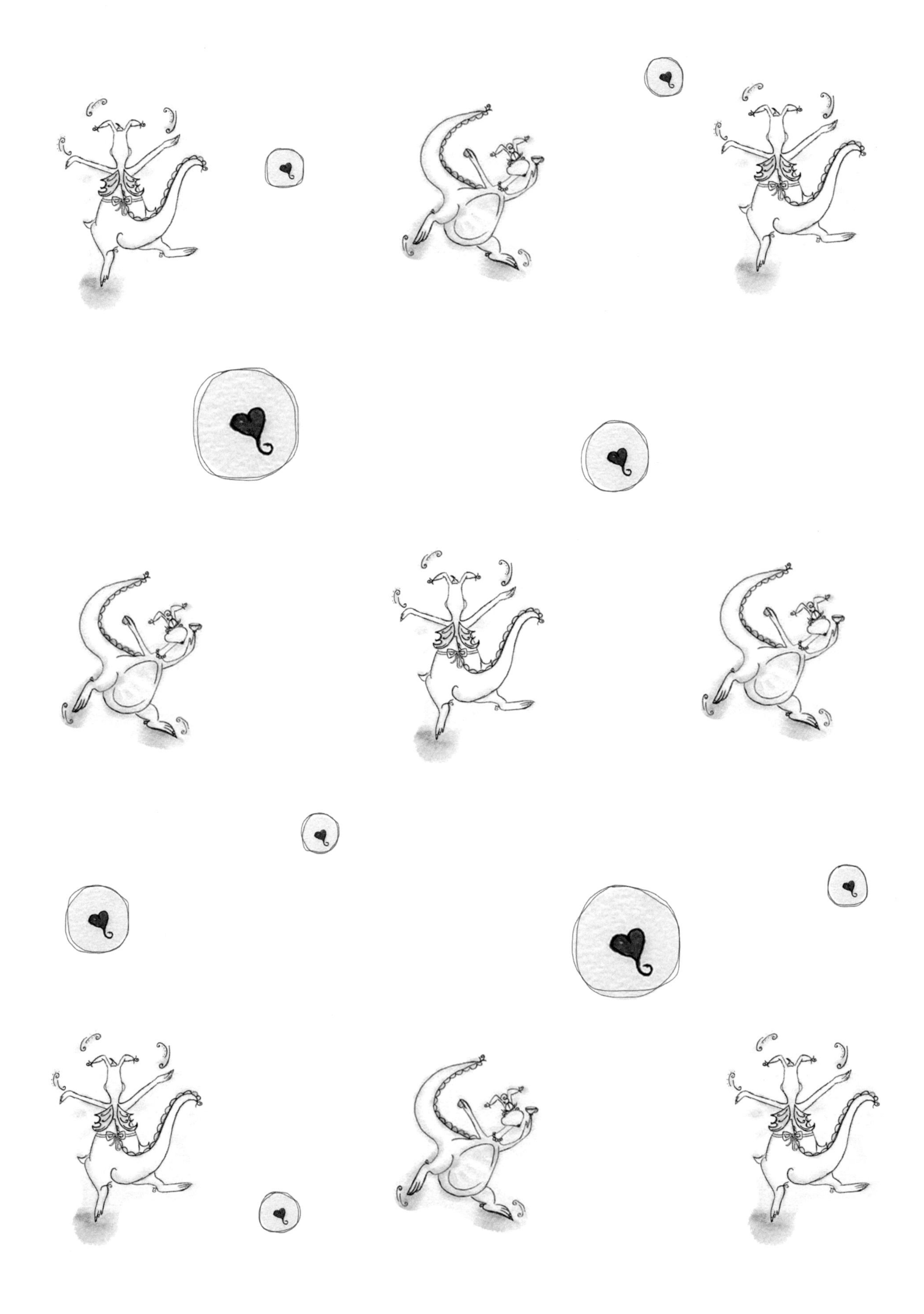

Made in the USA
Lexington, KY
09 September 2017